THE **ABC**s OF CRYPTIDS

Azdion Productions

Published by Azdion Productions

Azdion Productions
PO Box 7012
Kennewick, WA 99336

www.AzdionGalaxy.com

Printed by Artmil
www.Artmil.com

ISBN 978-0-615-43088-1

Library of Congress Control Number: 2010919115

Contents

Introduction

If you've picked up this book, you're probably either interested in cryptids (and why wouldn't you be?) or you're wondering what in the world a cryptid is.

Cryptozoology is the study of animals that are legendary, mythological, or otherwise not accepted in mainstream biology, often due to a lack of proof that they really exist. These creatures are called cryptids.

This book lists an alphabet of both notable cryptids, such as Bigfoot, and less commonly reported ones like the Ningen. Each entry features a fun artist's rendering of the cryptid and a few paragraphs about it. *The ABCs of Cryptids* isn't a very detailed resource, but it's a good starting place for those interested in these mysterious creatures.

Agogwe

The Agogwe is said to be a humanlike cryptid with reddish-brown hair and reddish-yellow skin (other colors of Agogwe have occasionally been reported). It is usually slightly smaller than a human, with long arms and opposable toes.

Sightings are rare, even for the natives of East Africa where the Agogwe was first spotted. The first sighting was in 1900 by Captain William Hichens, who didn't report it until 1937. After that, there were only a few more sightings.

Bigfoot

Bigfoot is possibly one of the most famous cryptids. It is reported to be a large, dark-colored ape which walks on two legs and appears very humanlike. Witnesses say it has a gorilla-like head with large eyes, and, of course, enormous feet.

Native American myths about creatures similar to Bigfoot have existed since long before the first sightings. Large tracks were discovered in 1951 and again in 1958, and since then some video and photograph footage featuring supposed Bigfoot creatures has surfaced.

Chupacabra

The Chupacabra (meaning "goat-sucker") is an infamous cryptid, usually thought to be some sort of reptile, but resembling a mix of a dog, porcupine, and even kangaroo. The creature's appearance varies widely depending on the source. It has fangs and is generally thought to be vampire-like.

The sightings began in 1995 when several sheep were found dead and drained of blood. Since then, countless livestock and pets around Puerto Rico, southern United States, and Mexico have been killed by these terrifying creatures, and many people have claimed to see it.

Dobhar-Chú

The Dobhar-Chú, or water-hound, is a water-dwelling cryptid. As the name implies, this cryptid resembles a dog or possibly a dog-like animal, such as an otter. It has flippers and is sometimes described as being part fish. It is apparently a very fast swimmer.

Myths of the Dobhar-Chú have existed in Ireland since the seventeenth century with the story of a woman being killed by one. Recent sightings are rather uncommon and there seem to be relatively few people who have witnessed it, but it may have played a larger role in Irish legend.

Elwetritsch

The Elwetritsch is a cryptid which resembles a chicken or other small bird, but has scales instead of feathers. It also has antlers and lives in the woods. It is apparently very curious, but rather timid.

The creature was discovered by a German man who promptly organized hunts for the animal. This involved a hunting party wandering into the woods, where one person would wait to catch the Elwetritsch while the others would coax it toward the catcher. This, however, and possibly the Elwetritsch itself, was a setup for a prank, because the others would leave the hunt and wait for the catcher to realize he was the only one still there.

Fouke Monster

Also known as the "Southern Bigfoot", the Fouke Monster is a terrifying apelike monster which enjoys killing and eating livestock. Witnesses say it is very large and has huge eyes that glow. Unlike the Bigfoot, it only has three toes and walks more similarly to an ape or a monkey than a human.

This cryptid was first reported in the town of Fouke, Arkansas in the early 1970s when it attacked a man at his house. According to local legend, though, the creature had been sighted since the 1940s. Sightings have continued somewhat frequently since the attack, and the monster has been blamed for dead and injured livestock and pets.

Giglioli's Whale

Giglioli's Whale is an identified species of whale. The primary difference between it and other whales is the fact that it has two fins on its back rather than one or none. There are also a few other differences, such as the appearance of its tail and throat. Other than this, it apparently resembles a rorqual-type whale.

The whale was discovered by Enrico Hillyer Giglioli in 1867 when he was on board a ship near Chile. He made a detailed diagram of the animal, but didn't try to bring the whale back with him. It was seen again a year later near Scotland, and the next (and last) sighting was in 1983 around France.

Huay Chivo

The Huay Chivo, meaning sorcerer-goat, is a cryptid described as being half-man, half goat, or a man that can turn into a goat. It occasionally has been described as turning into a dog or a deer. It has a reputation for attacking livestock and causing mischief, and may be associated with the Chupacabra.

The Huay Chivo is thought to relate to the Nahual of Mesoamerican folk religion; a person who could magically change into an animal. Unlike a Nahual, however, the Huay Chivo almost always uses its powers to cause harm.

Iliamna Lake Monster

The Iliamna Lake Monster is a gigantic fish, described as being anywhere from ten to thirty feet long. It is generally thought to be a huge sturgeon, but some think that maybe the monster is some other unknown kind of fish or even an undiscovered whale.

The monster has been seen off and on by fishermen around the large Iliamna Lake in Alaska. The monster has supposedly caused people to go missing, possibly by jumping out of the water and (accidentally or not) knocking them out of their boat.

Jackalope

A rather popular cryptid, the Jackalope is a species of hare that has antlers or horns growing from its head. People who have claimed to see the Jackalope claim a number of random facts about it, such as it being able to mimic human speech, and its meat tasting like lobster. It is usually aggressive.

The creature was first spotted in Douglas, Wyoming around 1829 and there have been many sightings since. President Ronald Reagan claimed to have shot a Jackalope, and mounted its head in his home. Although it is usually seen in North America, a similar animal has been spotted in some European countries.

Kraken

The Kraken is a sort of sea monster said to resemble a giant (forty or fifty feet) octopus or squid. It is very dangerous to sailors, as it can create a whirlpool by diving underwater which can suck ships in. It is also capable of pulling a ship underwater using its tentacles.

The Kraken is said to live around Norway and Iceland, and legends of octopus-like sea monsters have existed for a long time. The Kraken has been suggested as a cause for various ship disappearances, and was a somewhat popular cryptid around the 1800s and early 1900s.

Loch Ness Monster

Nearly as popular as the legendary Bigfoot, the Loch Ness Monster is a large serpent-like animal. Most of what is known of the animal is its small head and long neck. Some say there are humps on its back. Many claim that it appears similar to a plesiosaur, a type of dinosaur thought to be extinct.

It was first reported in early May, 1933, when a man and his wife encountered the monster while on the Loch Ness. In 1934, a blurry photograph of the beast was taken and sparked further interest. The Loch Ness Monster has gotten a lot of attention since then, and is an icon of cryptozoology.

Maltese Tiger

Although the tiger is definitely a real animal, the Maltese color variation of the species isn't confirmed to exist. The color is similar to the "blue" color in domestic cats, which is actually a shade of grey. The Maltese tiger still has regular black stripes, but they are over a grey coat instead of an orange one.

The first Maltese tiger was spotted in 1910 in China by a hunter named Harry Caldwell. There have only been a handful of sightings since then and no solid proof of such a color variation, but colors similar to the reported Maltese pattern have been observed in cheetahs, and the blue color is seen in many domestic cats.

Ningen

The eerie Ningen is a blubbery, whale-like creature which bears an uncanny resemblance to a human. It is large, and is usually reported to be pale in color. The most striking feature is its somewhat humanlike face, and also its humanlike arms and hands.

This cryptid has been reported only in recent years. It has been observed by the crews of whale research ships on a number of occasions, and mostly seems to dwell around the Antarctic regions. No solid evidence exists aside from artists' renderings and blurry photos.

Ozark Howler

The Ozark Howler is a large, intimidating cryptid. It is purported to be large and stocky, with a bear-like build (though some think the Howler might also be a sort of big cat). It has shaggy dark-colored hair and prominent horns, and a cry that sounds like a mix between a wolf howl and an elk bugle.

The Ozark Howler has supposedly been sighted around the states of Arkansas, Missouri, Oklahoma, and Texas. Unfortunately, there isn't much solid evidence of this strange animal other than eyewitness accounts and descriptions.

Phantom Kangaroo

Kangaroos are considered perfectly normal within their natural habitat. However, they qualify as cryptids when they show up far outside their habitat, in places where kangaroos aren't thought to live. These are known as Phantom Kangaroos.

There are or have been a handful of verified populations of kangaroos and wallabies which were kept as pets or escaped from zoos. However, there have also been sightings of Phantom Kangaroos (especially in the US) with no such explanation. At least one of the kangaroos sighted exhibited atypically violent behavior.

Queensland Tiger

The Queensland Tiger is usually described as a feline with a long tail and stripes, and it is described as being about the size of a dog. It is unknown if the Queensland Tiger is a kind of feral cat, or if it's a marsupial of some kind.

This animal lives around the Queensland area of Australia. There have been native traditions regarding this animal for a long time, but the first recorded sighting of a Queensland Tiger was in 1871. There have been reports since, but these have decreased since the mid 1900s.

Rat King

Rat Kings are described as a group of rats whose tails have somehow fused together. It has been reported to happen in many rat species, as well as mice and even squirrels. Some people believe Rat Kings are a bad omen.

Sightings have occurred as early as the 1500s, but have decreased in recent times. There is solid evidence of actual Rat Kings, in the form of mummified rats with their tails matted together, but recently the occurrence of Rat Kings seems to be decreasing.

Spring Heel Jack

Spring Heel Jack was a mysterious cryptid, thought to be a supernatural man or even a devil. He was often described as wearing a dark cloak and was said to have glowing eyes and the ability to breathe blue fire. He was famous for being able to jump very high.

The first report of Spring Heel Jack was in 1837 in London, when a man reported seeing him near a cemetery. He was spotted off and on in the next few years, and had a reputation for attacking or frightening women. The last sighting of Spring Heel Jack was in 1904.

Thunderbird

The Thunderbird is a large, mysterious flying animal named after the bird of Native American legend. Witnesses claim the animal has smooth skin, large bat wings, and a reptilian face. Some think it may be some sort of living pterodactyl.

The first sighting was reported around 1890, when two cowboys claimed to have killed a giant birdlike creature with featherless wings and a crocodile face. More sightings appeared throughout the 1900s and even as recently as 2007.

Umdhlebi

A rare plant example of a cryptid, the Umdhlebi is a supposedly poisonous tree. It has large, fragile green leaves on it and is said to have two layers of bark. The fruit that grows on the tree is red and black. The Umdhlebi might secrete a poisonous gas from its roots.

It was reported in 1882 by Reverend G. W. Parker, who saw the plant in South Africa. The native people would sacrifice animals to the plant to appease it, believing it was evil. Besides this report, no other people have claimed to see the Umdhelbi and no evidence of the plant exists.

Vegetable Lamb

The Vegetable Lamb is another plant cryptid. As the name implies, it looks similar to a sheep except for technically being a plant instead of an animal. It is connected to the main plant by an umbilical cord and it grazes on the surrounding grass.

It is thought that the idea of the vegetable lamb came about in medieval times as an explanation for where cotton came from. It has been referenced multiple times throughout recent history. The Vegetable Lamb is said to exist around Central Asia.

Will-o'-the-Wisp

Will-o'-the-Wisp is a rather unique cryptid. It appears as a ghostly flickering light over bodies of water such as swamps. The light usually has no apparent source. Some legends say Will-o'-the-Wisps are caused by fairies or ghosts, or perhaps some other paranormal activity.

Will-o'-the-Wisp is not a new cryptid, and has a place in many legends across the world. It always occurred over marshes, swamps, and bogs. Legends and reports of Will-o'-the-Wisp can be seen in Europe, Asia, and South America.

Extinct Animals

Extinct animals count as cryptids because, even though they were once real animals, they are no longer accepted as living species. Reports of living specimens of supposedly extinct animals can range from recently extinct animals to even dinosaur species.

Due to the diversity of extinct animals, listing sightings of all of them would take too long to write (and read!). Some commonly reported animals are the saber-toothed tiger, the thylacine (a carnivorous marsupial), and several species of wolf.

Yeti

The Yeti is an apelike or possibly even humanlike creature. It walks upright like a human and leaves large footprints, and witnesses have described it as having dark hair all over its body. The Yeti doesn't seem to be aggressive towards humans. It's similar to Bigfoot in many ways.

The first account of a Yeti sighting in the Himalayas was published in 1832, and a report of footprints appeared in 1889. Sightings and research have continued into the 1900s and as recently as 2008, but evidence of the Yeti is inconclusive.

Zuiyo Maru Creature

The Zuiyo Maru Creature was found as a carcass, but was described as looking much like a plesiosaur. It had a moderately long neck and tail, and four reddish-colored flippers. The corpse was decomposing, so little else could be determined about the creature.

The Zuiyo Maru Creature was picked up by a Japanese fishing trawler in 1977 near New Zealand. The crew didn't know what it was, but had to throw it back because it was decomposing and could contaminate the caught fish. Nobody has been able to find a living specimen of this creature.

About the Author

L. James is a freelance geek, and her interests are in art, writing, design, and sci-fi/fantasy. She's had an interest in cryptids ever since first learning about them, and loves them due to their often-fantastic nature and the possibility that they may be real. In her spare time she draws, writes, and plays around with web design.

About the Illustrator

Meg James is a (primarily) cartoon-style artist with an interest in fantasy. Having been interested in obscure and unconfirmed creatures for a while, she knew the cryptids featured in this book would be tons of fun to illustrate. Outside the cryptozoology field, Meg writes and illustrates her personal graphic novel-type works and pursues other artistic endeavors.